Jim Henson presents

The Christmas Toy

By Joanne Barkan Illustrated by Lawrence Di Fiori

Based upon the television show by Laura Phillips

No part of this publication may be reproduced in whole or in part, or stored in a retrieval system, or transmitted in any form or by any means, electronic, mechanical, photocopying, recording, or otherwise, without written permission of the publisher. For information regarding permission, write to Scholastic Inc., 730 Broadway, New York, NY 10003.

ISBN 0-590-40892-5

Copyright © 1987 by Henson Organization Publishing, Inc.
All rights reserved. Published by Scholastic Inc.

12 11 10 9 8 7 6 5 4 3 2 1

7 8 9/8 0 1 2/9

08

Printed in the U.S.A.
First Scholastic printing, October 1987

SCHOLASTIC INC.

New York Toronto London Auckland Sydney

It WAS CHRISTMAS EVE, and the weather was clear and cold. A thousand tiny stars lit the sky, and the moon draped a silver glow over the rooftops and the streets.

In the upstairs playroom of the Jones's house, the lights were still on. Jamie Jones was saying good-night to her favorite toy — a soft, furry tiger named Rugby.

Jamie gave Rugby one last hug, set him down next to the dollhouse, and then left the playroom.

That should have been the end of it until Christmas morning. But it wasn't. It was just the beginning.

The captain of the toy tugboat blinked his eyes. Then he peered out the playroom door through his telescope. When he saw that the coast was clear, he blew his whistle.

"It's time to play!" shouted Apple, a curly-haired, rosy-cheeked doll with real patent leather shoes.

Apple and the other toys in the playroom were always ready for fun as soon as the coast was clear. They loved to dance and sing and play a hundred different games and do everything else toys do when children aren't around.

But like all toys, they had to follow one rule. If they heard a real person coming, they had to jump back into place. Toys had to be found exactly where they had been left. If a real person caught a toy out of place, the toy would be frozen forever.

Balthazar, the bear, was the oldest and most experienced toy in the playroom. His fur was worn, and cotton stuffing poked out of his seams.

"I have important things to say," wheezed Balthazar as he slowly climbed to the top of the dollhouse.

Bleep, the robot, and Cruiser, the toy cab, helped the old bear up. All the other toys gathered around the dollhouse to listen. Rugby and Apple were there, and so were Ditz, the not-so-smart clown, and Ding-a-ling, the chatterbox telephone. Even the little catnip mouse named Mew wanted to hear what Balthazar had to say.

"Tomorrow," announced the bear, "is the most exciting day of the year for us. My dear friends, tomorrow is Christmas Day!"

"Christmas!" repeated Belmont, the spotted pony on wheels. "That means new toys in the playroom!"

"That's right," Balthazar nodded. "We must welcome these new members to our little community, and we must tell them about Christmas and the ways of the toy world."

"Christmas?" Rugby whispered out loud. "I didn't know Christmas was going to happen again."

"Well, then you'd better listen," warned Apple. "It's about time you found out how Christmas works."

"I don't have to listen," snorted Rugby. "I know all about it from last year. Christmas is about *me*. Whoopee! Everyone watches Jamie Jones open the box, and there I am, inside. Then the cheering begins, and Jamie says how much she loves me. Whoopee! I'm the bravest and greatest toy tiger around, and I'm the most important part of Christmas because I'm the *Christmas toy!*"

"Rugby," sighed Apple, "you're in for a big surprise.

But you're just too…too unbelievable for me to even try to explain." Then she turned away to listen to Balthazar.

Rugby Tiger paid no attention to Apple. He had something else on his mind. He glanced around once to make sure that no one was watching, and then he tiptoed to the playroom door. "I have to get downstairs to the living room and into my box. I'm the Christmas toy, and that's where I belong—in a box, under the tree."

Rugby peeked into the hallway. It was empty. Then he did something no toy had ever done before. Rugby stepped out of the playroom.

The hallway looked immense to Rugby, and it was dark. As he inched his way forward, it seemed like a long, long way to the top of the stairs that led down to the living room.

"This isn't scary at all," Rugby muttered a few times as he tried to get his legs to stop shaking. "After all, I'm the bravest and the greatest—"

Suddenly the door to one of the bedrooms opened, and the hall was flooded with light. Rugby gasped, but he couldn't move. He didn't know what to do.

Mr. and Mrs. Jones appeared in the doorway. "How many other families do you think are doing laundry on Christmas Eve?" Mr. Jones asked.

Mrs. Jones laughed. "All the families with sloppy kids and a house full of relatives expected tomorrow."

Rugby looked up just in time to see a pile of towels and sheets and shirts sailing his way. The next thing he knew, he was buried underneath the Jones's laundry.

"Help! Emergency! Hey, listen to me!" Mew, the little catnip toy, was trying desperately to get the other toys' attention. "Something bad has happened! You've got to help! Help!"

Apple wrinkled up her nose. "Pew! It's Mew! Well, what's the matter?" she demanded.

"Rugby," panted Mew. "He shouldn't have done it. I know he shouldn't have. He left the playroom!"

Everyone gasped.

Old Balthazar moaned, "He'll be frozen."

Belmont closed his eyes and shook his mane. "How could Rugby do something so stupid?"

"Stupid?" asked Ditz, wagging his clown's head from side to side. "What's so stupid about that? Let's just stick our heads out the door and call Rugby back."

Before anyone could stop him, Ditz lurched to the door on his wobbly legs and poked his silly head out. He was leaning against the door when—without warning—Mrs. Jones pushed it open and walked in. Ditz fell right on top of her foot.

"Lots of laundry in here," sighed Mrs. Jones, "and a toy to trip over, too." With one hand she gathered up dirty socks and jeans, and with the other hand she tossed Ditz into a corner of the playroom. He landed with a sad thud.

As soon as Mrs. Jones had gone, the toys ran over to their friend. Apple rubbed his hands and patted his cheeks. Balthazar examined his eyes. But there was nothing to be done. Ditz was frozen.

"I had hoped we'd never have to see this again," mourned Balthazar, his eyes misted over with tears.

The toys lifted the limp doll and placed him carefully in the open car of the toy train. The whistle blew, and they walked alongside the clown as he made his final trip around the playroom. The train came to a halt, at last, next to the shelves where several other frozen toys sat as still as stones.

Meanwhile, little Mew paced back and forth, talking to himself. "They've forgotten all about Rugby! What if the same thing happens to him? I've got to do something. Rugby is my hero. He's the bravest and greatest toy around—just like he always says."

Mew stopped pacing for a moment. "Of course, he also always says that I smell and that catnip makes him sneeze. And he doesn't think I'm much of a toy because I'm just a cat toy, not a people toy." Mew started pacing again. "But who cares what he says. He's still my hero."

It was very quiet in the playroom. The other toys were still too shocked and frightened to act.

"Well, I'm not waiting," thought Mew. "I'm going to rescue Rugby now."

None of the toys noticed when Mew dashed out of the playroom door.

Rugby Tiger poked his head out from under the laundry pile. He looked around quickly and then stood up.

"Lucky that Mrs. Jones didn't notice me!" he said to himself. "Now I've got to get downstairs and—"

Rugby sniffed the air. "That's a familiar smell." He whirled around, and there was Mew. "Mew! Pew!" Rugby sneezed twice. "What are you doing here?"

"I've come to rescue you," squeaked Mew.

"*You* rescue *me?*" Rugby hooted. "You're not even a people toy. You're a cat toy. Anyway"—Rugby ran to the top of the stairs and peered down into the living room—"I've got important things to do—like get into my box under the tree so that Jamie can find me again. After all, I'm the Christmas toy!"

All of a sudden, Rugby's ears perked up. There were footsteps just inside one of the bedroom doors. Rugby took a deep breath, balanced on his back paws, and then threw himself down the stairs. Mew had no choice but to somersault after him.

In the middle of the living room stood the Christmas tree. The Joneses had trimmed it with gold and silver balls and tiny colored lights that reflected off the walls and floors like jewels. The tinsel glittered, and little brass horns and bells hung from the branches.

"It's like magic," whispered Mew.

Rugby nodded. "It's just the way I remembered it." Then he shook himself. "Time to find my box."

Under the tree, there were boxes of every size and shape. Mew and Rugby examined several before they found a box that had Jamie's name on the tag. Rugby tried to pull off the top, but it was held in place by a wide pink ribbon. "Now what do I do?" groaned Rugby, whose tiger cub paws were not nimble enough to untie the bow.

"Never fear when Mew Mouse is here!" Mew piped up. Swinging by his tail from a low branch on the tree, Mew managed to undo the ribbon with his teeth.

"Not bad." Rugby nodded in approval. "Not bad at all for a cat toy." Then he bent over to open the box.

"Rugby! Don't!" Apple stood at the top of the stairs, looking down into the living room. Belmont, Bleep, and Cruiser, the cab, were with her. The four brave toys had ventured out of the playroom in the hope of rescuing Rugby and Mew.

Apple was frantic. "We've got to get them back to the playroom. But if there's any noise, we'll be caught and frozen." She jumped aboard the cab. "To the Christmas tree!" she ordered. "And step on it!"

Belmont and Bleep remained on the landing as guards while Cruiser bounced down the stairs with Apple. Rugby was still struggling to open the box when Cruiser slammed on his brakes under the tree. Apple ran over to Rugby.

"Rugby, you can't get into that box!"

"Why not?" Rugby retorted. "Because you want to get in? You're just jealous because I'm the Christmas toy."

Apple threw up her hands. "I don't want to get into that box because I've already been there, Rugby. I was the Christmas toy the year before you were. You can do it only once, and then the next year, there will be a new toy."

"I don't believe you," sniffed Rugby.

"Well, then," sighed Apple, "look in the box."

Rugby pulled off the box top and peered inside. His eyes opened wide.

Lying in the box was a new doll, a tall, slender doll, dressed like a space warrior and carrying a laser sword.

"Wow," breathed Mew. "Just look at her!"

The doll awakened suddenly and sat up. "I am Meteora," she announced with a flourish of her sword, "Queen of the Asteroids." She glared at Mew. "Take me to your leader, you sorry excuse for a grizbot."

When the startled toy didn't respond, Meteora leaped out of her box and strode off in the direction of the chessboard that sat on the coffee table.

Apple turned to Rugby. "Now do you understand?"

"Oh, I get it all right," muttered Rugby. "I was Jamie's Christmas toy after you, and this Meteora thing is Jamie's Christmas toy after me. Only I won't give up without a fight! Maybe I'll—"

CRASH! Something heavy fell to the floor, and the sound echoed through the quiet room. The toys looked around in panic. There was Meteora—standing in the middle of the chessboard, waving her laser sword. She had just knocked one of the ivory knights to the floor and was threatening the king.

"Tuldon, King of the Megadors!" she thundered, "prepare to meet your doom!" Without a moment's pause, Meteora whipped her sword through the air and knocked

the chess king to the floor. CRASH! The other toys froze in horror.

"What was that?" Mrs. Jones's voice came from the upstairs bedroom. "There's something in the living room."

"I'll go see," answered Mr. Jones.

Footsteps padded across the bedroom floor. The door started to swing open.

"I guess this is the end for us," Apple murmured.

"I'm sorry, everybody," whispered Rugby.

Just then, Mew puffed out his little chest and squealed, "Meeooww." It was a long, high-pitched meow that sounded exactly like the Jones's cat. Mew did it a second time. "Meeeooowww."

Mr. Jones stopped in the doorway. "It's nothing," he called out to his wife. "Just the cat." He shut the door and walked back across the bedroom floor.

The toys stared at one another in disbelief. It seemed like a miracle. Thanks to Mew, they hadn't been caught and frozen.

"That was fantastic!" Apple gave Mew a big hug.

"Not bad at all!" agreed Rugby.

"Not bad for a cat toy?" Mew wanted to know.

Rugby looked Mew over from the top of his ears to the tip of his tail. "Not bad for *any* toy," he replied.

The toys in the living room solved their next problem without too much difficulty. They coaxed Meteora back into her box by promising that when she awoke again she would be the center of attention under the Christmas tree.

Then Apple, Rugby, Cruiser, and Mew made their way up the stairs as swiftly and quietly as they could. At the landing, Apple and Bleep climbed onto Belmont's back. Rugby jumped aboard Cruiser, and little Mew

clung to the end of Rugby's long tail. They took off at top speed, racing down the hallway. Just one moment more and the toys would be safely back in the playroom.

"Hold on, Mew!" warned Rugby as they careened around the corner near Mr. and Mrs. Jones's bedroom.

"I can't!" Mew wailed, feeling his grip on Rugby's tail loosen. "I'm slipping!" Mew grabbed frantically at the air as he lost hold of Rugby and slid to a stop in front of the bedroom door.

Belmont and Cruiser reached the playroom without
realizing what had happened.

"Mew fell off!" cried Rugby.

He was about to run back down the hallway to help
Mew when they all saw the door to the Jones's bedroom
open again. Mrs. Jones switched on the light. Mew lay
trembling at her feet.

"I can't believe we forgot to turn off the Christmas tree lights." Mrs. Jones shook her head as she stepped out of the bedroom. "And look at this," she added, scooping up Mew. "That cat of ours is as sloppy as the kids!"

Mrs. Jones walked downstairs to the living room, dropped Mew into the cat's basket, and turned out the tree lights. Then she returned to the bedroom, shutting the door behind her.

As soon as the bedroom door closed, Rugby stepped into the hallway. The other toys could do nothing to stop him.

"I have to talk to Mew," he insisted, "even if he's frozen now and can't hear me."

Rugby crept slowly down the hallway. "There's so much to tell him, things I should have told him before." The toy tiger wiped away a tear and started down the stairs. "Mew, you were the best friend I ever had, but did I ever thank you? Oh, no! Never. Now I want to tell you that…that I really like the smell of catnip."

Rugby tiptoed cautiously into the living room. "Mew?" He caught sight of the catnip toy lying upside down in the cat's basket where Mrs. Jones had dropped him. Rugby ran over and gently turned Mew rightside up.

"What I really want to say, Mew…" Rugby leaned over and whispered in the frozen toy's ear. "What I really want to say is that I love you."

The words were magic.

Rugby's eyes were filled with tears, and so he didn't notice Mew start to move—first his whiskers and then his ears. In just another minute, Mew was stretching as if he had awakened from a long, deep sleep.

"Mew!" Rugby shrieked. "You're alive!"

Mew looked confused. "It was all so strange," he said. "At first, I was very cold, then it got warmer..."

Neither Rugby nor Mew could explain what had happened. So they hugged each other tight, agreed that it

must be Christmas magic, and promised to be best friends forever.

When they got back to the playroom, they found another puzzling but equally wonderful surprise. Ditz, the clown, and all the other frozen playthings had come alive again. Yet not one of the rejoicing toys — not even old Balthazar, the bear — understood how it had happened. All they were ever able to find out was this: At precisely the moment when Rugby leaned over and whispered in Mew's ear, the frozen toys began to move.

It was midmorning on Christmas day. All the presents had been opened, and the Jones family was finishing breakfast. Upstairs, Meteora and the other new toys were being introduced to the playroom and to the ways of the toy world. The captain of the toy tugboat stood guard at the playroom door. The coast was clear.

"I can tell you all about Christmas," Rugby announced to Meteora. "I'm an expert. Christmas is about...it's about friends. Yes, it's all about old friends and new friends and being together." Rugby stopped for a moment, and then he added, "So Christmas is really about every one of us. Isn't it?"

Old Balthazar nodded his head as he walked over to the window. When he looked outside, the first snowflakes were drifting down. They were large, heavy flakes that settled one by one on the window ledge. They soon covered the rooftops and the streets with a crystal blanket.

It was going to be a perfect Christmas day for all the Christmas toys.